MW01265140

This Book
Belongs To:

To Lorne & Mary White
Dad & Mom

You have shown me that it is important to be true to myself. Thank you for your example and love .

Forever I'll Be Thankful

Forever I'll be Thankful, Second Edition
Copyright © 2016 by Holly M. Roddam. All rights reserved.

This title is also available as a Tate Out Loud product. Visit www.tatepublishing.com for more information.

Published by Tate Publishing & Enterprises, LLC
127 E. Trade Center Terrace | Mustang, Oklahoma 73064 USA
1.888.361.9473 | www.tatepublishing.com

Tate Publishing is committed to excellence in the publishing industry. The company reflects the philosophy established by the founders, based on Psalm 68:11,
"The Lord gave the word and great was the company of those who published it."

Book design copyright © 2016 by Tate Publishing, LLC. All rights reserved.
Cover and Interior design by Eddie Russell
Illustration by Kurt Jones

Published in the United States of America

ISBN: 978-1-68028-807-0
Juvenile Fiction: Family: Parents
15.11.26

Little Child of God

Forever

I'll be Thankful

Second Edition

written by
Holly M. Roddam

tate publishing
CHILDREN'S DIVISION

My mommy and daddy love me.
I get kisses all day long.

And if I fall down,
they pick me up
And cheer me with a song.

They feed me fruit and veggies.
No "fast food" stuff for me!
Just salmon, peas and
blueberries,
My very favorite three.

I love Mommy and Daddy,
And that is why, you see,
Forever I'll be thankful
For all their love for me.

Heavenly Daddy loves me,
He sent me a present one day.
A little baby, just like me
To take my "boo-boos" away.

The baby's name was Jesus,
And when He grew to be a man,
He showed us how
to live for God
By following His plan.

"For God so loved the world, that He gave
His only Son, that whoever believes in Him
should not perish but have eternal life."

John 3:16 (RSV)

I love my Heavenly Daddy.
In His home one day I'll be.
And forever I'll be thankful
For His great love for me.

"My Father's house has many rooms.
If that were not true, would I have told
you that I'm going to prepare a place for
you?"

John 14:2 (GW)

I have so many blessings
That I really want to share
With others who have nothing,
Or don't know Jesus' care.

So if I can be a blessing
By giving others love,
Then I will do it gladly
Just like Heavenly Daddy does!

I love that I am learning
This very important key,
"As long as I am thankful,
Love and joy is what I'll see!"

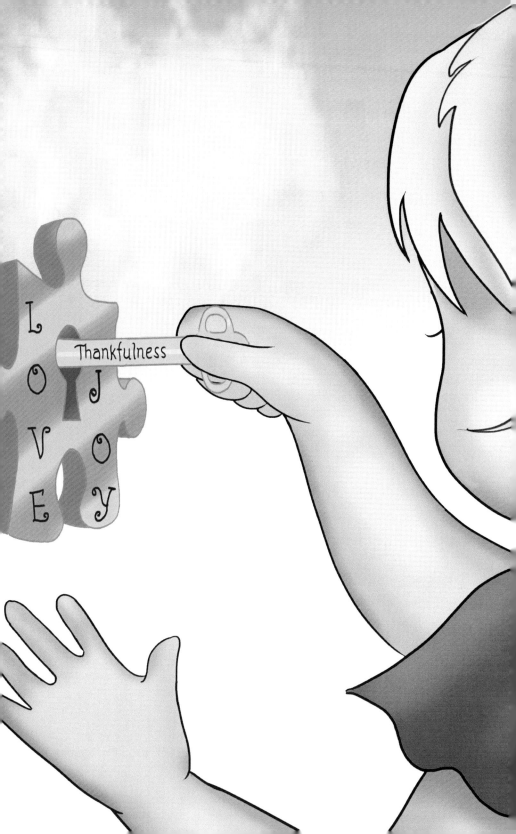

I may be little, but that's OK!
If I follow the Saviour
in every way,
I'll make a difference
as long as I live,
And forever, I'll be thankful!

Note to parents and caregivers from the author

It has been my joy to know Jesus since I was a child. I learned about Jesus in Sunday School, but He was more than an historic figure or a person in the Bible stories. Jesus was my friend. We talked all day every day. I have cherished this my whole life.

I "got saved" when I was nine because my eleven-year-old friend told me that if I asked Jesus to forgive my sins I would go to Heaven when I died. Jesus and I were already best friends and I wanted to be where my best friend lived 😄.

When John and I had our own children, it was very important to us to introduce them to Jesus when they were children too. By then we had become acquainted with the Holy Spirit, so we introduced them to Him as well. Children are so open to the things of the Spirit. If they can meet Jesus at an early age, they will have the pleasure and benefits of walking with God their whole lives long.

My prayer is that my books will help children of all ages know that God loves them and has a wonderful plan for their lives. He wants us to know that plan and has given us His Word and the life of Jesus to help us find it. If I can help children understand what it means for them to be a "Little Child of God", to see that they don't have to wait to "grow up and be old enough" to follow Jesus, then I will have done my job.

Like Jesus' parables, I hope the easy to read and memorize story verses will find a place in the hearts and spirits of your children, and the truths conveyed inform their earthly journey. I have included scriptures and questions to be a springboard for further discussion about what it means to be a follower of Jesus.

I would love to know if my books have helped you share Jesus with your little ones, or where they could be improved. I want to give my best so that children can know the Lord. You can leave comments on my web site, http://hollyroddam.tateauthor.com or email me at hollyroddam@live.com. I will attempt to answer everyone who writes me.

Let's raise up a generation who will bow down and worship Jesus, the Christ, as Lord and King in their lives, and shine like stars in the universe as they hold out the Word of Truth for others to see. The more they know about the truth of who God is, the more they will be able to say, "Forever I'll Be Thankful for His great love for me!"

Peace & Love,
Holly M. Roddam <><

Note: Don't try to do this all at once. Take time each day to read through the story verse so your child can learn it. Then focus on one particular aspect of the story and talk about what it would look like for your child to live out the Truth of God's Word in his or her life today. You might want to spend more than one day on certain aspects. However you do it, have fun! It's because of God's great love for us that we can know Him, so enjoy our Heavenly Daddy.

Peace & Love,
HMR <><

ဢဢ✝ဢဢ✝ဢဢ✝ဢဢ

1

Mommy and Daddy love me.
I get kisses all day long.
And if I fall down, they pick me up
And cheer me with a song.

- What do your mommy and daddy do that makes you FEEL loved?

- What do you do to show love for your mommy and daddy?

- Do you like to sing? Singing is a good way to cheer yourself up if you are sad or scared. Did you know that God sings too? He sings because He is happy! He loves you very much and is delighted with you. He watches over you and is always with you so you don't have to be afraid. If you listen, maybe you will even hear Him singing joyful songs over you.

Memorize Zephaniah 3:17.

"For the LORD your God is living among you. He is a mighty savior. He will take delight in you with gladness. With his love, he will calm all your fears. He will rejoice over you with joyful songs." Zephaniah 3:17 NLT

ಐಲ✝ಐಲ✝ಐಲ✝ಐಲ

2

They feed me fruit and veggies.
No "fast food" stuff for me!
Just salmon, peas and blueberries,
My very favourite three.

- God cares a lot about what we eat, where we live and how we are doing. You can tell that He cares about us because He looks after all the birds of the air and the fish in the sea and makes sure that they have enough to eat. If He cares about the birds and the fish, just think how much more He cares about you! Read about it in Matthew 6:25-34.

- Memorize Matthew 6:26 and 14:14.

"Look at the birds. They don't plant or harvest or store food in barns, for your heavenly Father feeds them. And aren't you far more valuable to him than they are?" Matthew 6:26 NLT

Though Jesus wanted solitude, when He saw the crowds, He had compassion on them, and He healed the sick and the lame. Matthew 14:14 VOICE

- Jesus cared a lot when there was a great crowd of hungry people. Only one little boy had brought food with him. Jesus took that food, thanked God for it and shared it with over 5000 people. And everyone was full! Jesus can look after us when we are in need too. Read the Bible account of how Jesus fed everyone with a miracle in Matthew 14:13–21 below. In your own Bible, read about another time that Jesus fed people in Matthew 15:29-39.

Disciples: We're in a fairly remote place, and it is getting late; the crowds will get hungry for supper. Send them away so they have time to get back to the villages and get something to eat.

Jesus: 16 They don't need to go back to the villages in order to eat supper. Give them something to eat here.

Disciples: 17 But we don't have enough food. We only have five rounds of flatbread and two fish.

Jesus: 18 Bring the bread and the fish to Me.

So the disciples brought Him the five rounds of flatbread and the two fish, 19 and Jesus told the people to sit down on the grass. He took the bread and the fish, He looked up to heaven, He gave thanks, and then He broke the bread. Jesus gave the bread to the disciples, and the disciples gave the bread to the people; 20 everyone ate and was satisfied. When everyone had eaten, the disciples picked up 12 baskets of crusts and broken pieces of bread and crumbs. 21 There were 5,000 men there, not to mention all the women and children.   *Matthew 14:13-21 The Voice (VOICE)*

- Read how John told this same story in John 6:2-14 in your own Bible.

ಖಐ✝ಖಐ✝ಖಐ✝ಖಐ

3

I love Mommy and Daddy,
And that is why, you see,
Forever I'll be thankful
For all their love for me.

• What are some of the things mommy and daddy do for you?

They cook meals, love you, wash your clothes, pray with you, play with you, teach you about Heavenly Daddy and Jesus, go to work to earn money to buy your food and clothes.

Have you said, "Thank you!" to them today for all that they have done?

• Make a list of 5 things people do to show their love for you.

1. _____

2. _____

3. _____

4. _____

5. _____

• Thank Jesus for these things. Add to the list each day. See how many new things you can add. Don't forget to continue to thank God for the first things on your list.

• When you are thankful and obedient to your parents, you honor them. This is one of the 10 Commandments God gave His children when He brought them out of slavery. This was the first commandment with a promise attached to it. God said if you obey your parents, you will live a long and happy life. When we practice obeying our parents we are also obeying our Heavenly Daddy who wants only the best for us.

- Memorize Eph 6:1-3

   Children, obey your parents as you would the Lord, because this is right. Honor your father and mother, which is the first commandment with a promise, so that it may go well with you and that you may have a long life in the land. Eph 6:1-3 Holman Christian Standard Bible

- If you have not obeyed your parents or haven't been thankful for them, ask Jesus to forgive you. Then tell your parents you are sorry and ask them to forgive you too. If we ask for forgiveness, God will forgive us every time.

   Memorize 1 John 1:9 and James 1:22. Don't forget to do what it says!

   If we confess our sins, he is faithful and just to forgive us our sins, and to cleanse us from all unrighteousness. 1 John 1:9 King James Bible

   Do what God's word says. Don't merely listen to it, or you will fool yourselves. James 1:22 God's Word Translation

ೞಞ✝ೞಞ✝ೞಞ✝ೞಞ

Note to parents: I have broken this section into 3 parts. There are some heavy concepts here. Take some extra time with your child to make sure they understand what God has done for them in giving us Jesus, and how your child can accept this gift and have eternal life. – HMR <><

4

Heavenly Daddy loves me.
He sent me a present one day.
A little baby, just like me,
To take my booboos away.

Part 1

- The Bible talks a lot about Jesus being born. Here are a few verses you can look at to get you started to see just how much God loves us and what He did for us.

*²¹And she will bring forth a Son, and you shall call His name **JESUS**, for He will save His people from their sins.²²So all this was done that it might be fulfilled which was spoken by the Lord through the prophet, saying: ²³"Behold, the virgin shall be with child, and bear a Son, and they shall call His name Immanuel," which is translated, "God with us."* Matt 1:21-23 NKJV

- Why did God send Jesus to earth?

> *⁶For unto us a Child is born,*
> *Unto us a Son is given;*
> *And the government will be upon His shoulder.*
> *And His name will be called*
> *Wonderful, Counselor, Mighty God,*
> *Everlasting Father, Prince of Peace.*
>
> *Isaiah 9:6 NKJV*

- Jesus has a lot of names! Each one tells something wonderful about who He is and how He loves us. Talk about the names of Jesus listed in Isaiah. Do you know any other names for Jesus? As you read your Bible, look for new names and see what they tell you about who Jesus is.

ॐ ☩ ॐ ☩ ॐ ☩ ॐ

Part 2

- God is LOVE. He loves us so much that He wants to us to be with Him forever and ever. The Bible says we *all* do things wrong and make "booboos". When we tell 'little white lies', or are mean, or disobey our parents, it is sin. Every time we sin, we fall short of God's plan for our lives. This separates us from God, just like when a criminal breaks the law and is arrested. He is put in jail cell away from everyone else.

  All have sinned and fall short of the glory of God. Romans 3:23 NIV

- God knew we would make mistakes but He didn't want us to be separated from Him forever. But someone had to pay the penalty for our sins. So God came up with a plan! *HE* would pay the penalty Himself so we wouldn't have to be separated from Him forever. The only way for us to get out of prison is to let Jesus pay the penalty for us and ask God to forgive us.

  16 For God so loved the world that He gave His only begotten Son, that whoever believes in Him should not perish but have everlasting life. 17 For God did not send His Son into the world to condemn the world, but that the world through Him might be saved. John 3:16-17 NKJV

- Why do we need to be forgiven? What are we being "saved" from?

ଈଓଔ☦ଈଓଔ☦ଈଓଔ☦ଈଓଔ

Part 3

- God became a person by being born as a baby. Jesus is God with skin on! He was just like us, but with one big difference. He NEVER did anything wrong! That meant He didn't have to pay for His own sins, so He could pay for ours. This is why Jesus came – to save us from *our* sin.

  This is a trustworthy saying, and everyone should accept it: "Christ Jesus came into the world to save sinners..." 1 Timothy 1:15 NLT

- When Jesus was beaten, nailed to the cross, died and was buried in the tomb, it was like He went to jail for us. He paid for all the mistakes or bad things we will ever do. But when He came back to life and rose from the dead, He broke the power that sin, disobedience and doing wrong had over us. If we ask Jesus to forgive us, and believe He died for us, we won't have to give in to the power of sin. We can say "NO!" and live like Jesus instead. We will also know the joy of being forgiven and will never have to go to jail for eternity. Instead, we will go to live with Jesus.

  "My Father's house has many rooms. If that were not true, would I have told you that I'm going to prepare a place for you?" John 14:2 God's Word Bible (GW)

- If you would like to accept Jesus' gift to you, pray this prayer and you will be born again. Jesus will forgive you and come to live in your heart.

Dear Jesus,

Thank You for coming to earth as a baby and growing up without doing anything wrong. I am sorry that I make booboos and do wrong. I want to be a *Little Child of God* and follow God's Word, just like You did.

I don't want to pay for my sins myself. I want to live with You forever. Please forgive me. I accept your gift of salvation. Please come into my heart and save me. Send Your Holy Spirit to live in me and help me to live for You.

Whenever I do make mistakes, please remind me that if I ask, You will forgive me, and You will help me to not do it again.

I love You Jesus, and thank You for saving me. Thank You that I will live with You all the days of my life, and when I die, I will go to live with You in Heaven.

In Your Name I pray,

Amen

ಐ ೦೪ ✝ ಐ ೦೪ ✝ ಐ ೦೪ ✝ ಐ ೦೪

5

The baby's name was Jesus,
And when He grew to be a man,
He showed us how to live for God
By following His plan.

- Jesus grew up following God's laws and obeying His parents. When Jesus' family went to the Temple in Jerusalem, He gave His parents a scare! Read what happened and how Jesus honoured God and His parents.

Jesus Speaks with the Teachers

[41] *Every year Jesus' parents went to Jerusalem for the Passover festival.* [42] *When Jesus was twelve years old, they attended the festival as usual.* [43] *After the celebration was over, they started home to Nazareth, but Jesus stayed behind in Jerusalem. His parents didn't miss him at first,* [44] *because they assumed he was among the other travelers. But when he didn't show up that evening, they started looking for him among their relatives and friends.*

[45] *When they couldn't find him, they went back to Jerusalem to search for him there.* [46] *Three days later they finally discovered him in the Temple, sitting among the religious teachers, listening to them and asking questions.* [47] *All who heard him were amazed at his understanding and his answers.*

[48] *His parents didn't know what to think. "Son," his mother said to him, "why have you done this to us? Your father and I have been frantic, searching for you everywhere."*

[49] *"But why did you need to search?" he asked. "Didn't you know that I must be in my Father's house?"* [50] *But they didn't understand what he meant.*

[51] *Then he returned to Nazareth with them and was obedient to them. And his mother stored all these things in her heart.*

Jesus grew in wisdom and in stature and in favor with God and all the people. Luke 2:41-52 (NLT)

- When God created us He had a special plan in mind - to love Him and know Him as our loving Heavenly Daddy. Sometimes we think we can live any way we want to, but that is not the way God made us.

  Think about how silly it would be to try to bake a cake in a washing machine. You could put the eggs, milk, flour and sugar in the tub and the agitator would stir them up, but if you tried to get the batter out to put it in the oven, you would just have a big mess inside the washing machine! A washing machine was made to wash clothes, not mix cake batter!

  Just like the washing machine was made for a certain purpose, God designed us to do wonderful things in the world that would bring Him honor and glory, and would help us to know Him better. It would be just as silly for us to try to live without God as it is to try to mix a cake in the washing machine!

- There is a booklet that tells you how to use the washing machine correctly and there is a book that tells us how to live. Did you know God had a book out? It's the Bible! He wrote The Bible so we would know how to live.

- Memorize Ps 119:105

  Your word is a lamp for my feet, a light on my path. Ps 119:105 NIV

- Jesus came as a human being to show us what living the Bible looks like. We can look at His life, read His Word and know what God's plans are for our lives. The wonderful thing about following Jesus is, the more we walk in His footsteps the better our own life will be. If we follow God's plan, we will grow up to be like Jesus and be a blessing to others. Because God created us, *He* knows what we need to do to get the most out of life.

- Memorize these verses to remember God has a plan for us.
  "For I know the plans I have for you," declares the LORD, "plans to prosper you and not to harm you, plans to give you hope and a future." Jeremiah 29:11 NIV

¹⁰ It is God himself who has made us what we are and given us new lives from Christ Jesus; and long ages ago he planned that we should spend these lives in helping others. Eph 2:10 LB

There is a way that seems right to a man, but the ways therein end in death. Prov 19:17

- God wants us to follow Jesus' example and do what the Bible says. If we read the Bible and memorize it, we will know how to obey God and live the exciting, wonderful life He has planned for us. Read the stories of Jesus' life in the Gospels: Matthew, Mark, Luke and John. See how He behaved and treated people. Ask yourself, "What would Jesus do if He was me?" Then, do it ☺.

- Memorize this verse:

I have hidden your word in my heart, that I might not sin against you." Ps 119:11 (NLT)

- The best part about following Jesus is that we don't have to do it alone. Jesus promised He would always be with us, even after He went back to Heaven. Jesus sent the Holy Spirit, the third person of God, to live in us so He could help us. Make sure you get to know Him too!

Jesus Promises the Holy Spirit

¹⁵ "If you love me, you will keep my commandments. ¹⁶ And I will ask the Father, and he will give you another Helper, to be with you forever, ¹⁷ even the Spirit of truth, whom the world cannot receive, because it neither sees him nor knows him. You know him, for he dwells with you and will be in you." John 14:15-17 ESV

๒ଊ✝๒ଊ✝๒ଊ✝๒ଊ

6

I love my Heavenly Daddy.
In His home one day I'll be,
And forever I'll be thankful
For His great love for me.

• Do you ever think about what it will be like to go to Heaven and live with Jesus forever? The Bible tells us what Heaven is like. It is more beautiful than anything we have ever seen. It is full of people who love God and Jesus and each other. There is no sickness or sadness in heaven.

"He will wipe every tear from their eyes. There will be no more death or mourning or crying or pain, for the old order of things has passed away." Revelation 21:4-8

• Did you know that Heaven is NOISY?! There are millions of angels worshiping and praising God all the time. Crashing cymbals and all kinds of musical instruments are playing praises to God. Even lightning and thunder praise the Lord. It is a *JOYOUS*, noisy party. I think some grownups think Heaven is like a quiet park, but they're going to be surprised!

"And I heard a sound from heaven like the roar of mighty ocean waves or the rolling of loud thunder. It was like the sound of many harpists playing together." Rev 14:2 NLT

"After this I heard what sounded like the roar of a great multitude in heaven shouting: "Hallelujah! Salvation and glory and power belong to our God," Rev 19:1 NIV

"Then I heard what sounded like a great multitude, like the roar of rushing waters and like loud peals of thunder, shouting: "Hallelujah! For our Lord God Almighty reigns."
Rev 19:6 NIV

- Heaven will be a great place to be because everyone is happy , and playing, and praising, and loving, and being loved ! I can hardly wait to go! . I hope I see you there. Oh yes! and there *WILL* be dancing !

- But the very best thing about Heaven is that Jesus is there!

- *"1 Let not your heart be troubled. You believe in God, believe also in me. 2 In my Father's house there are many mansions. If not, I would have told you: because I go to prepare a place for you. 3 And if I shall go, and prepare a place for you, I will come again, and will take you to myself; that where I am, you also may be."*
  John 14:1-3 (DRB)

ഊരു✝ഊരു✝ഊരു✝ഊരു

7

I have so many blessings
That I really want to share
With others who have nothing,
Or don't know Jesus' care.

- God made Abraham a promise. He said He would bless him so that Abraham could bless the whole world.

Abram and Sarai
[1] GOD told Abram: "Leave your country, your family, and your father's home for a land that I will show you. [2-3] I'll make you a great nation and bless you. I'll make you famous; you'll be a blessing. I'll bless those who bless you; those who curse you I'll curse. All the families of the Earth will be blessed through you." **Genesis 12:1-3** *The Message (MSG)*

- When God gives us gifts and talents, He wants us to do 3 things with them:
  1st use them to make Him happy.
  2nd use them to help others.
  3rd be blessed by them ourselves and see them as gifts that we can enjoy.
- God made every single person with special talents. Some people are really good at sports. Others are very creative and are good at things like singing and acting or drawing. Others have the ability to run companies and be successful business people. Did you know that even little children can start a company and bless others?

At 6 years old, Jonas Corona, Chief Changer/Founder of *Love in the Mirror* used his abilities for good. You are never too young to do good. Watch http://loveinthemirror.org/.

Hart Main, age 13, turned helping the homeless into a business!

 ManCans are made with real soup cans bought from a local grocery and donated to a soup kitchen. The empty can is returned, cleaned and made into candles. Hart is feeding people who need a little extra help.

www.man-cans.com

- Jesus said, "Let the children come to me. Don't stop them! For the Kingdom of Heaven belongs to those who are like these children." **(Matt 19:14 NLT)**

Meet Martin Zÿlstra, a 10 year old evangelist! Martin knows Jesus as his friend and wants all his classmates to know Jesus too. At 9 years old, he joined the Gideon program, *Send Me*, www.sendme.ca and received free Bibles from the Gideons to give his classmates. He shared his desire to win his whole school over for Jesus on YouTube. http://www.youtube.com/watch?v=Tbq_9zwOajk

- There are a few children in the Bible that you might like to read about:

- The Little Captive Maid & Naaman: Read 2 Kings 5:1-15b
  … the girl said, "If your husband Naaman would go to the prophet in Samaria, he would be cured of his leprosy." 2 Kings 5:3 CEV
  A child tells her master how to get healed.

- Josiah: Read 2 Kings 22:1- 23:23
  *Josiah was eight years old when he became king of Judah… ²Josiah always obeyed the LORD, just as his ancestor David had done. **2 Kings 22:1-2 CEV***
  King Josiah discovered that his people had not been obedient to God. The king cleansed the land of idolatry and encouraged worship of God only.
- **Samuel: Read 1 Samuel 1-3**
  ¹⁰The LORD then stood beside Samuel and called out as he had done before, "Samuel! Samuel!" "I'm listening," Samuel answered. "What do you want me to do?" 1 Samuel 3:10 CEV
  Samuel obeyed God from the time he was a child and the Lord blessed him.

- The boy who gave his loaves and fishes to Jesus: Read John 6:1-15
  9 "There is a boy here who has five small loaves[a] of barley bread and two fish." John 6:9a CEV

  Jesus can use whatever we have to do miracles and make us a blessing to others.

- **Timothy**

  15 Since childhood, you have known the Holy Scriptures that are able to make you wise enough to have faith in Christ Jesus and be saved. 2 Timothy 3:15 CEV

  Timothy's grandmother, Lois, and mother, Eunice, taught him the great things God had done from the time he was very young. He learned the Word of God and became a pastor.

- **David vs Goliath: Read 1 Samuel 17:1-50**

  36 "Sir, I have killed lions and bears that way, and I can kill this worthless Philistine. He shouldn't have made fun of the army of the living God! 37 The Lord has rescued me from the claws of lions and bears, and he will keep me safe from the hands of this Philistine." 1 Samuel 17: 36, 37 CEV

  David spent time with God while watching the sheep. He knew God and how He could help him.

- **The Holy Child Jesus (see *"Jesus Speaks with the Teachers"* in section 5)**

  Even Jesus didn't wait to be a grown up to serve God.

- Work on the things you can't do well so you will get better at them. Just like exercising your muscles makes them grow, when we practice doing good, our spirit grows big and strong and we get good at doing good!

  There is a saying, "Practice makes perfect." It means if you practice long enough you will do something perfectly. But that is only true if you practice the right way! It would be better to say, "Practice makes *permanent*." However you practice, that is how you will always do it! So make sure you practice doing good and you will do good all the time.

- Celebrate how God has made each of us unique and special. Encourage your friends in the things they do well. We are all different. Just because someone can't do something as well as you doesn't mean they are any less of a person, or unworthy of being loved and valued. It just means that you are different from each other. Maybe they can do things that you cannot. No one can do everything well except Jesus! God made us all with different gifts, so we would need each other.

ഇൻ✝ഇൻ✝ഇൻ✝ഇൻ

8

So if I can be a blessing
By giving others love,
Then I will do it gladly
Just like Heavenly Daddy does!

- What is a blessing?
  A blessing is an act or word that imparts power to make someone's life better in some way. When we bless someone, we share God's love and ask Him to smile on them.

- The very first thing God did after He created Adam and Eve was to bless them so they could look after the Garden of Eden and all the animals. He blessed them with "dominion" or authority and power over all the creatures on earth.

  [28] Then God blessed them, and God said to them, "Be fruitful and multiply; fill the earth and subdue it; have dominion over the fish of the sea, over the birds of the air, and over every living thing that moves on the earth." NKJV Genesis 1:28

- How can *you* be a blessing?
- When you compliment or congratulate someone, you encourage and empower them to do it again. It makes them feel good about themselves.
- You are a blessing when you do things out of the goodness of your heart not expecting anything in return. You could open a door for a disabled person or buy a homeless person something to eat or be just be nice to your brother or sister!
- When you notice someone doing or saying something nice, tell others about it. This will bless the person doing good, and show others the good in that person.
- When you bless your enemy, it can turn him or her into your friend! Jesus said, *"Love your enemies and pray for anyone who mistreats you. Then you will be acting like your Father in heaven." (Matt 5:44-45a).*

- **God is Love.** When we love, we are being like Heavenly Daddy. We can love everyone, even those who are hard to love, if we love them with God's love. He loves us whether we are naughty or nice, and we can love others the same way.

Jesus taught us *The Golden Rule* for how to treat others. *"Treat other people exactly as you would like to be treated by them—this is the essence of all true religion."* Matthew 7:12 PHILLIPS

- Most people don't want to be mean, but sometimes sad things happen to hurt them inside, and they act out of that hurt. Sometimes people are hard to love because no one has ever blessed them or encouraged them to be the best they can be. But when we love them with Jesus' love, God uses that love to change and heal them. It is amazing how you can turn a person's day right side up with just a hug and a smile. Try it!

- Read Matthew 5:43-48b

- When we ask Jesus to forgive us our sins, the Holy Spirit comes to live in us and we are given power to be like Jesus. Jesus loves us and told us to *"Love one another as I have loved you."* (John 13:34). Because the Holy Spirit lives in us, we are blessed and can obey this command.

- We can love Jesus by loving those He loves. Jesus said if you are kind to someone *"... no matter how unimportant they seemed, you did it for me."* (Matt 25:40 CEV)

Are there any people in your neighborhood who don't have friends or enough to eat? Ask the Lord how you can make a difference in their life. Is there an elderly person who is lonely? You could give a hug to the elderly person whose grandchildren live in a different city and let them be your grandparent for the day! You could make muffins or a lunch basket with your parents and take it to a shut in or someone who is sick.

- Think of three things you can do today to be a blessing to someone else. There are many needs around us. You can ask God to bless you to be a blessing at any age!

- **Read Matthew 25:31-46**

- Memorize these verses

"In the same way, let your light shine before others, so that they may see your good works and give glory to your Father who is in heaven." Matthew 5:16 ESV

"Treat others the same way you want them to treat you.." Luke 6:31 NAS

For we are his workmanship, created in Christ Jesus for good works, which God prepared beforehand, that we should walk in them. Ephesians 2:10 ESV

Imitate God, therefore, in everything you do, because you are his dear children. Ephesians 5:1 NLT

Don't repay evil for evil. Don't retaliate with insults when people insult you. Instead, pay them back with a blessing. That is what God has called you to do, and he will bless you for it. 1 Peter 3:9 NLT

Instead, we will speak the truth in love, growing in every way more and more like Christ, who is the head of his body, the church. Ephesians 4:15 NLT

- We are to have the same character as God, our Heavenly Daddy, and love people like He does. He will use our love and kindness to be His hands and feet.

  Casting Crowns has a song about this called **"If We Are the Body"**. You might like to listen to it on YouTube (https://www. youtube.com/watch?v=9_7j1SMuTN0) and learn it to remind yourself that you are the Body of Jesus to your friends and neighbours.

ꮡ ꮯ ✝ ꮡ ꮯ ✝ ꮡ ꮯ ✝ ꮡ ꮯ

9

I love that I am learning
This very important key,
"As long as I am thankful,
Love and joy is what I'll see!"

- There are so many verses in the Bible about being thankful, especially in the Psalms. When we are thankful we are open to receive more. When we are grumbling about all the things we don't have or didn't get when we wanted them, sometimes we don't see all the things that we already have!

6 Don't worry about anything; instead, pray about everything. Tell God what you need, and thank him for all he has done. 7 Then you will experience God's peace, which exceeds anything we can understand. His peace will guard your hearts and minds as you live in Christ Jesus. Philippians 4:6-7 NLT

Be thankful in all circumstances, for this is God's will for you who belong to Christ Jesus. I Thessalonians 5:18 NLT

The Lord is my strength and shield. I trust him with all my heart. He helps me, and my heart is filled with joy. I burst out in songs of thanksgiving. **Psalm 28:7** New English Translation (NET)

You have turned my mourning into joyful dancing. You have taken away my clothes of mourning and clothed me with joy, 12 that I might sing praises to you and not be silent. O LORD my God, I will give you thanks forever! Psalm 30:11-12 NLT

- When we have an attitude of gratitude, we can see how we are blessed. Even when we are in the worst of situations, we can be happy that there is still something for which to be thankful.

- Make a list of 5 things for which you are thankful. Add at least one new thing to the list each day. You will soon see there are many things for which to be thankful.

1. _____

2. _____

3. _____

4. _____

5. _____

- Here is a great way to learn Psalm 30:11-12. Go to Ron Kenoly's song "Mourning Into Dancing" on YouTube: https://www.youtube.com/watch?v=cE6GstI1FKc. When you see all the things you can thank Jesus for, I bet you'll say this too: "*I can't stay silent. I must sing for His Joy has come!*" I bet you'll have to dance for joy too!

- Ask your mom or dad if you can have some old magazines to cut up. Cut out pictures of all the things for which you are thankful and make a collage or poster. Hang your poster in a place where you will see it each day. It will remind you to thank Heavenly Daddy for all His love for you.

- Make a little sign with **Philippians 4:6-7** on it and stick it on the mirror you look at in the morning. This will remind you give your day to Jesus. Then get ready for a big adventure with Him!

ॐ✝ॐ✝ॐ✝ॐ

10

I may be little, but that's OK!
If I follow the Saviour in every way,
I'll make a difference as long as I live,
And forever, I'll be thankful!

- You may think you are too little to do something great for God. But sometimes grownups are too big for God to use and He needs the help of a child. We read some Bible stories of children who worked with God, and saw some children from today who are doing great things for God. We just have to be willing for God to use us, and He can make amazing things happen! You can even silence your enemies!

From the mouths of little children and infants, you have built a fortress against your opponents to silence the enemy and the avenger. Psalm *8:2 GW GOD'S WORD Translation*

- Jesus told grownups that unless they humbled themselves and became like little children, they would not be able to understand God, Heaven or even how to live the best life here on earth! You have the ability now to believe Jesus' words and follow Him. Adults have to learn how if they didn't learn it as a child. So don't sell yourself short (pardon the pun)! In the book of Matthew, Jesus spoke very seriously to adults who were trying to keep children from Him.

[2]Jesus called a small child over to him and set the little fellow down among them, [3]and said, "Unless you turn to God from your sins and become as little children, you will never get into the Kingdom of Heaven. [4]Therefore anyone who humbles himself as this little child is the greatest in the Kingdom of Heaven. [5]And any of you who welcomes a little child like this because you are mine is welcoming me and caring for me. [6]But if any of you causes one of these little ones who trusts in me to lose his faith, it would be better for you to have a rock tied to your neck and be thrown into the sea. Matthew 18:2-6 Living Bible *(TLB)*

[13]One day some parents brought their children to Jesus so he could lay his hands on them and pray for them. But the disciples scolded the parents for bothering him. [14]But Jesus said, "Let the children come to

me. Don't stop them! For the Kingdom of Heaven belongs to those who are like these children." ¹⁵*And he placed his hands on their heads and blessed them before he left.* Matt 19:13-15 NLT

- God will teach you by His Holy Spirit and the Bible what you need to know to grow into the person He created you to be. Then you will be able to walk out your destiny in Him and change the world.

- Memorize these verses so you will remember that God is your teacher.

  All your children will be taught by the LORD, and great will be their peace. **Isaiah 54:13** NIV

  "When, however, the Spirit comes, who reveals the truth about God, he will lead you into all the truth. He will not speak on his own authority, but he will speak of what he hears and will tell you of things to come." John 16:13 GNT Good News Translation

  ¹⁵ *From infancy you have known the Holy Scriptures. They have the power to give you wisdom so that you can be saved through faith in Christ Jesus.* ¹⁶*Every Scripture passage is inspired by God. All of them are useful for teaching, pointing out errors, correcting people, and training them for a life that has God's approval.*

  ¹⁷ *They equip God's servants so that they are completely prepared to do good things.* **2 Timothy 3:15-17** God's Word Translation

- When Jesus called His disciples, many of them were teenagers. They left everything they were doing to follow Jesus. He taught them how to "fish for people instead of fish" and be His witnesses. He wants to teach you how to "catch your friends" and introduce them to Him too.

  Jesus said to them, "Come, follow me! I will teach you how to catch people instead of fish." Matt 4:19 GOD'S WORD Translation

- If we love Jesus we should obey His commandments. There are still millions of people who don't know how much Jesus loves them. He wants us to help tell them.

"If you love me, obey my commandments. John 14:15 NLT

And Jesus came and said to them, "All authority in heaven and on earth has been given to me. Go therefore and make disciples of all nations, baptizing them in the name of the Father and of the Son and of the Holy Spirit, teaching them to observe all that I have commanded you. And behold, I am with you always, to the end of the age."
Matthew 28:18-20 ESV

- Living with Jesus is an adventure every day. There is always someone you can talk to about Jesus and His love. This little poem reminds us that some people will never hear about Jesus unless we tell them. Memorize it, then remember to live like Jesus. If you do, you'll make a difference as long as you live, and that is something for which to be thankful!

You're writing a gospel a chapter a day
By the deeds that you do
and the words that you say.
Men read what you write,
distorted or true!
What is the gospel
according
to
you
?

-Anonymous